CITY OF MARTYRS

CONNOR WHITELEY

No part of this book may be reproduced in any form or by any electronic or mechanical means. Including information storage, and retrieval systems, without written permission from the author except for the use of brief quotations in a book review.

This book is NOT legal, professional, medical, financial or any type of official advice.

Any questions about the book, rights licensing, or to contact the author, please email connorwhiteley@connorwhiteley.net

Copyright © 2023 CONNOR WHITELEY

All rights reserved.

DEDICATION
Thank you to all my readers without you I couldn't do what I love.

CHAPTER 1

My rebellion cannot die.

As much as I love to think that, I know at some point all my friends, rebels and everyone I love will die or be killed. My job is to make sure that happens as far into the future as I can, which is why I'm in this godforsaken place.

The sound of peasants walking in the mud, talking and laughing with the other peasants filled the air as I looked down at them from the high window that I carefully hid behind.

As a female assassin I don't have anything against peasants and everyday people, I was once one of them, and some peasants did look after me time from time after the Overlord killed my Assassin siblings and forced me to go on the run.

But I have never understood how they can find live quietly at peace whilst the Overlord and its servants make their lives a living hell. I don't understand why these people don't stand up and fight for their freedom.

For example there's a woman down there who is being shouted at by some Overlord Guards in their horrid black armour that I would happily slice through, but is she saying anything? Is she defending herself? Is she doing anything that would make these men think twice?

No.

And that is why I do what I do, I want to defend the innocent, protect them and make sure my life is worth living. Yet I also suppose that's why I joined the silly rebellion with their damn values, cause and heroics.

I saved them once, they loved them and gave me a family of sorts, so now I feel like I have to protect them.

The horrible smell of poo, urine and rotten food fills the air as I realise what one of the nearby buildings below was used for, I didn't want to be here any longer than necessary.

If I wasn't on official business then I would never have stayed here for as long as I have (four hours), but if I was ever going to free the Kingdom, kill my father the Overlord (don't judge) and protect the rebellion, then I needed to do something here first.

I went away from the window and went over to the large wooden door that was the only entrance to this place. I hated the formal hard wood floors and walls to this office and its small official desk that was far too grand for purpose.

How I didn't smash it up the moment I got here I didn't know. But soon everything would be destroyed because I needed to kill this Governor.

Lord Governor Marisia of Outpost Ova was nice my favourite of people, if you asked anyone (including the Rebellion who meant to know all these things) they would have told you she was a rich woman who donated thousands to the poor each week, and she was one of the best Governors in the Kingdom, ruling over her district with fairness, justice and righteousness.

Rubbish!

Whereas if you were an Assassin (like wonderful old me), then you knew her as a cold, calculating, cunning killer. I first heard of her when I was a contract killer and she hired me to kill a hundred peasants because… I quote… *I don't want to feed those extra mouths.*

Not exactly the worse reason I've ever been hired but it does come close.

Anyway I'm going to stab her with my two long swords, and she needed to die now because apparently she had learnt the location of the rebellion, and I wasn't going to allow her to kill my friends for love, money or spite.

The sound of footsteps came from the hallway behind the door and I pulled my black leather cloak and hood tighter as I prepared to strike.

The door opened.

Lord Governor Marisia walked in with a massive smile on her face. I hated her straight away with her long pompous robes, her stunning jewel and her perfectly done hair.

This was the image of a woman who didn't care about anyone else, if she had then she would have focused more on her people and not herself.

The door shut. I heard the guards walk away.

I went up to her. Placing my blades firmly against her throat.

"I wasn't expecting the Assassin Protectorate of The Rebellion," she said.

I know I got that title a month ago, being the Protectorate of the Rebellion, but I really don't like it. It sounds pompous, arrogant and like I'm far superior to my station. I so wasn't going to let her say that again.

"You know Assassin, your friends have made a lot of progress along the St Julian's Way,"

As much as I needed to spill her blood now, I felt as if I had to know how much she knew, the Rebellion had mentioned taking that path towards the so-called Holy Sections of the Kingdom, but that was silly. The Overlord ruled those lands directly, no one would help them there.

"Relax Assassin, I haven't sent the orders yet and I presume I never will now. But there is something far better waiting for you," she said with a smile.

I pressed my swords harder into her throat.

"The Overlord has activated them again. The

Hunters will come for you and the Rebellion. They will find you, kill you and deliver you to the Glorious Overlord,"

Damn!

That is not what I wanted. I couldn't have those silly, stupid half-human, half-demon shadowy monsters after me. I had enough trouble with them last night.

Damn it!

I needed more time. I needed to meet up with the Rebellion, plan our next moves, we were ruined after the Overlord attacked us, slaughtered our forces and forced us to move bases.

We didn't have any fighting power left, we couldn't fight back, we were barely surviving. And that is what I wanted to change.

"Don't worry *Lord* Governor, I will kill you. I will make sure you're found. Then I will save the Rebellion, find a City and we will kill the Overlord,"

Marisia shook her head. "The Hunters will stop you. You won't get far,"

I moved closer to her ear. "Then we'll go to the one place they would never dare step foot inside,"

Marisia gasped. "The City of Martyrs?"

I had no idea that was where they couldn't go. I was making it up based on some stories I'd heard years ago but at least I knew where the Hunters would come for me now. Hopefully that City would help me and my friends rebuild, regroup and take the fight to the Overlord.

I didn't want any more unneeded deaths.

"Yes," I said.

Marisia struggled. "That is Holy ground. That is outrageous. That-"

I slit her throat, threw her body out the window and escaped to meet up with the Rebellion. I had to warn them about the Hunters.

CHAPTER 2

Commander Coleman stared at the two rows of the bloodied injured men and women that laid before him as the carriage rode along the long twisting road ahead.

Coleman had hated leaving their base over a month ago but there was no other choice. The Overlord knew where they were and unlike the Rebellion's forces, the Overlord had unlimited numbers of soldiers at his disposal.

It was only because of the Assassin's quick thinking that had bought them enough time to escape.

The Assassin was stunning with her amazing body, long black hair and her deep dark eyes that Coleman wished he could stare into every day.

He didn't want to keep thinking like this but he had to. Coleman loved the Assassins that much was fact, but he didn't know how to talk to her, show her his affection and develop whatever was between them into a relationship.

But it didn't take a genius to know that the Assassin probably wasn't into a relationship, especially with Coleman. Especially after Coleman had apparently tried to control her or be overprotective, he still hated himself a little for even trying such a thing. But love definitely made him do stupid things.

Especially towards one of the most beautiful, kick-ass women he had ever met.

The quiet sounds of moaning, coughing and hissing reminded Coleman of the horrific losses the Rebellion had suffered and it wasn't like most of these injured soldiers would heal or survive. The Rebellion didn't have those sorts of supplies.

Coleman had tried to reach out to allies but none of them were interested. As far as those so-called allies were concerned, the Rebellion was dead, long live the Overlord.

That sentence alone was disgusting and Coleman didn't understand how these people could so easily live under that foul Overlord's tyrannic rule.

Coleman was more than glad that his father had rescued him from the City of Pleasure as a teenager. He didn't want to become a sex slave for some Noble or Monarch, he wanted to be free.

But now he was, he had to free others.

The smell of blood, disease and damp filled the air and Coleman didn't like any of it. He wanted better for his people, he wanted to show leadership, courage and that he had a master plan. But he didn't. Coleman had failed as a leader, a fighter and now he was leading his friends on the run.

That was no way for a Rebellion to fight, too weak to defend themselves, much less attack the Overlord.

But at least Coleman had one weapon. He didn't like to think of his beautiful Assassin as a weapon, but at this point he didn't have a choice, the Assassin was the only advantage the Rebellion had.

If anything happened to her, then the Rebellion was truly dead (and so was Coleman's heart).

A man with a blood spattered face and covered in bandages weakly raised his arms towards Coleman, he went over to the man. He smelt awful with hints of sweat, blood and sick assaulting Coleman's nose.

"Closer," the man said weakly.

Coleman knelt on the ground and put his ear close to the man's mouth.

The man's arm moved.

A blade sliced through the air.

Coleman shot back.

The man jumped up.

Ran at Coleman with the blade.

A gunshot went off.

The man dropped down.

Coleman looked to see who the shooter was and Coleman was relieved to see it was a tall woman with her wonderfully smooth face, long blond hair with a smile that always lit up the room.

It was one of the few people in the entire world that Coleman trusted automatically. It was Abbic. And considering that her sister had betrayed the Rebellion a month ago and almost killed them all, Abbic was doing rather well.

"Alright their Bossie?" Abbic asked.

Coleman looked at the corpse. "I am now, thank you. Tell security to double check everyone again. That's the ninth attempt this month. There can't be that many traitors still here,"

Abbic's smile melted away. "Ma sis was traitor enough so anything possible me Lord,"

Coleman gave her a nod of respect and wished he could do or say more to her. He didn't want anyone to be in pain but clearly her sister's betrayal had scarred her. Coleman couldn't blame her really, they were close and as much as Coleman didn't want to admit it, her sister was a close friend.

Abbic started to walk away but stopped. "Me Lordie, tha Assassin's back,"

Coleman couldn't believe his luck and for the first time in a month, he smiled. He truly smiled. Coleman felt as if the tides were turning in his favour, but most of all he was just looking forward to seeing the woman he loved.

CHAPTER 3

I wasn't impressed in the slightest as I felt the horrible carriage jerk, bump and jump in the air as the entire Rebellion travelled along the massive long road ahead of them.

All I wanted was a good gently ride to our destination, which I don't think even the Rebellion knew where they were going. That alone was why I had returned, to warn them and hopefully give them some kind of direction.

I stood in front of a silly little wooden table with some maps, documents and unlit candles covering it. I presume this table had once been used as a way to plot their course and note down the various intelligence reports me and my "agents" (if you can call them that) had sent the Rebellion over the past month.

But now like the rest of the Rebellion, the table had been reduced to scraps and eroded by the constant grind of the journey.

The sounds of people talking, coughing and splattering wasn't the best of sounds to hear considering what was coming. These Rebels would last five minutes against the Hunters or any sort of major attack by the Overlord.

There were few options left for us, but I had to leave them for a time. That was the clearest one. My blood Father The Overlord would always focus on hunting me over the Rebellion, so if I went, it would at least buy them a few more days.

The smell of mould, damp and spoiled ale filled my senses as I looked up at the man standing opposite me.

Coleman's right hand man Dragnist kept staring at me and smiling. It wasn't creepy or anything but it was like he was obsessed with me. Granted his long black beard, killer smile and scar covering his face had a certain attractive quality to them. I wasn't interested in him.

I did like Coleman though.

I wanted Coleman to get here so I could tell him my news and hopefully help him lead.

The entire reason why I had left for the past month was simple, I didn't want to see him in his crippling pain of self-perceived failure, hate and disappointment.

The door opened behind Dragnist and Abbic with her perfectly long straight blond hair walked in and stood next to me. Then I saw my beautiful Coleman with his amazing dark emerald eyes, fit body and… his stunning smile was gone.

A small smile formed on his lips when he saw me but it was nothing compared to the smiles I got before the Overlord attacked, slaughtered and almost ruined the Rebellion.

I had to change that.

I pulled my black leather cloak and hood tightly over myself and nodded at Coleman.

"Come on Assassin, what ya gone for us?" Abbic asked.

Under my hood I smiled. "Where are we heading?"

Coleman tried to smile but he couldn't. "Holy Section of the Kingdom. We have-"

"Turn back Coleman. Everyone in those lands will kill us. Everyone serves the Overlord. We have no allies there,"

Coleman shrugged. I hated seeing him like this.

"Ha. Assassin, we don't have any allies. The Rebellion is defeated, dead, useless," Coleman said.

I shook my head. "Dragnist, report,"

Dragnist physically shivered as I said his name.

"Yo girl, ten percent of surviving Rebs are fighting strength. Rest are injured,"

The problem with being the cold calculating assassin I'm known of is it makes me very glad to have my hood hiding my face, as I know for a fact that my face was horrified at that number.

But that's the problem. Because I'm the Rebellion's and the entire Kingdom's only hope for survival, freedom and peace, I can't show my horror. I have to be strong or everything is lost.

"I killed the Lord Governor," I said.

Coleman let out a breath.

"Thank ya!" Abbic said jumping in the air.

"That might have bought you a week at least. But the Hunters are returning for us. Their mission apparently is to kill me, you and the Rebellion," I said to Coleman.

He didn't even react.

I really didn't like how bad he had gotten. I wanted to support him, lead with him and show… and show how much he meant to me. But I couldn't love anyone in this much self-hatred.

"What do you all know about the City of Martyrs?" I asked.

Coleman, Dragnist and Abbic just stared at each other. Then looked back at me.

"Yo Assassin, we ain't going there,"

"Na to that," Abbic said.

I looked at Coleman.

He looked at me. "The City of Martyrs is one of the most fortified Cities outside the Capital. No one goes there. No one lives there, not really. No one… survives going there,"

"What is it?" I asked.

Abbic came over to me and placed a hand on my shoulder. I forced myself not to react.

"Ta City of Martyrs is a church City. The High Priestesses and Priests and Synagogue live there. The entire City is dedicated to ta Overlord,"

I smiled at the sound of that. I do love killing, I love killing Religious figures even more.

"Ta City isn't friendly. Religious rules over tha people-"

Coleman tapped the table. "Wait! But no one likes the Religious leaders. The Leaders keep such an iron grip on the City that the people are terrified of them. They want the Rebellion there. I received message after message years ago from them. Then nothing,"

I leant over the table. "Why?"

Coleman shrugged. "Unknown,"

I stood up straight and turned to leave. "Ready me a horse. I'm going to the City of Martyrs. We're going to free it, kill the Religious Leaders and save the Rebellion,"

Coleman gave me a mocking laugh. I just glared at him.

"Assassin you can't do that. The Rebellion-"

"Be silent Coleman! The Rebellion isn't dead. The City of Martyrs is filled with people who hate the Overlord. People that want to be free. People that can heal, feed and fight for us!"

His eyes lit up at that.

I went over to him. "Please, Coleman come with me,"

He smiled. "Fine. You, me and Abbic can go. Dragnist you're in charge. Abbic knows the City well from her... what do call it,"

"I call it ya studies. I studied that City like I did my magic area when I was 16. I know everything about it,"

That was just disturbing.

I smiled at all of them under my hood. "We leave in half an hour. We ride to the City of Martyrs, free it, kill the leaders and claim it for the Rebellion,"

Everyone nodded.

I pointed a finger at Dragnist. "Be at the City in six days,"

I didn't want to put a countdown on my mission, but I had to make sure the Rebels were safe, secure and alive.

Everyone nervously nodded.

And with that, I realised we only had six days to loosen the Overlord's iron grip on a City or the Rebellion would truly die.

That scared me more than anything.

CHAPTER 4

Commander Coleman was relieved to know the Rebellion still had some friends left in the Kingdom as he sat on the bow of a small fishing ship that was heading for the City of Martyrs.

There was always something breathtakingly magical about sailing in the dead of night with the bright stars shining in the cloudless sky and the full moon guiding their way.

Coleman had always loved sailing, boats and the sea ever since his father had rescued him from the City of Pleasure all those decades ago, and despite the freezing cold night Coleman still loved the sea just as much.

Coleman ran his fingers along the smooth cold wood of the bow and stared at the beautiful glassy sea below as the ship surged towards their destination.

The City of Martyrs could be the true death of the Rebellion, but at this point Coleman didn't care. There were no more options left, regardless of what the beautiful, stunning Assassin said.

If anything this pointless attempt to invade, capture and free the City was just an excuse so Coleman could die meaningfully. He didn't want to think like this but that was the cold, hard truth of the Rebellion.

And the sooner the Assassin learnt that the better.

Coleman didn't even understand why she was still here. The Assassin could go on with her life, live happily and free in the Kingdom. But instead she chose to die with the Rebellion.

Whether that was brave, stupid or a mixture of the two Coleman hadn't decided yet, but he wanted to protect her as much as he could.

The sounds of the waves crashing against the ship, the creeping of the ship and the muttering of crew members reminded Coleman how alone the Rebellion truly was.

Once the Rebellion travelled on loud noisy warships filled with thousands of angry people shouting, screaming and demanding their revenge against the Overlord. Now there were basically none.

Coleman wanted the old times to return.

The sound of someone sitting next to him made Coleman look up and stare into those perfect dark eyes and imagine that perfect body under the long black cloak and hood of the Assassin.

He wasn't sure if he wanted to talk to her, he already knew she thought of him as pathetic, weak and not a leader. So should he make his situation worse in her eyes?

"I have missed you Coleman,"

Coleman's mouth dropped. He hadn't been expecting that. He was expecting some demanding pet talk but in front of him was a kind, gentle woman that actually wanted to support him.

"I missed you too," Coleman said, knowing how lame it sounded.

"I had heard reports but I didn't know the Rebellion was this bad,"

Coleman wanted to shout some dramatic defence about how grand and valour the Rebels had fought. But he never ever wanted to lie to the Assassin, so he realised he could only tell her the truth.

"A few days after you left they found us. They kept coming wave after wave after wave. We... we were almost slaughtered again,"

The Assassin looked out to the sea. "I'm sorry for leaving,"

Coleman cocked his head. "It wasn't your fault. I charged you with being our Protectorate and you did that. You went after threats that could have ended us,"

The Assassin still didn't look at Coleman. He was starting to wonder if there was something she wasn't telling him.

"What's the plan?" the Assassin asked.

Coleman checked if they were alone and leant closer. He savoured the smell of her delicious coconut scented hair.

"There was an old friend of my fathers who ran a pub in the City. We head there. Investigate it. Hopefully he will still be alive,"

"If not?"

Coleman shrugged. "Then we find a new base and go from there,"

The Assassin laughed. "Okay, you do that. I've got another thing I want to look into,"

Coleman felt the hairs on his arms stand up. Had he disappointed her? Coleman hated the idea of being weak or not doing the right thing in her eyes, but this was what he knew to be right.

If he could just find his father's friend then they would be safe to conduct their business in the City without any risk of discovery.

"You do that. I know what I'm doing. You can meet us at the pub," Coleman said before realising how demanding he was being.

The Assassin nodded, pointed behind him and walked away.

Coleman felt the sweat roll down his spine as he looked behind him, he hoped he hadn't annoyed her.

But when he looked behind himself, his eyes widened as the stunningly beautiful City of Martyrs. For miles upon miles up and down the coastline stretched thousands upon thousands of little candles stretching as far back as they did long.

It was like hundreds of thousands of people were standing their perfectly still with a candle to light the way for any ships coming.

It was stunning.

Coleman didn't know how to describe but his eyes narrowed on the true marvel of the entire City. All the hundreds of thousand of lights were designed in such a way that the massive golden dome in the centre of the City was lit bright.

It must have been a cathedral or important place because it was the focal for the entire thing and Coleman loved it.

Except for how terrifying the entire effect was, in a way Coleman supposed it looked like a massive army with their impressive command station standing firm against all passing invaders.

But unlike those perceived passing invaders, Coleman and his friends weren't passing. They were invading and Coleman swore he was going to invade, conquer and free the City no matter the cost.

CHAPTER 5

This is far from the best killing ground I've visited.

This is utterly ridiculous because how the hell am I meant to kill people without others seeing me!

Take this long cobblestone road up the hill me, Coleman and Abbic are walking up, there are so many candles lighting up the cobblestone that it might as well be daylight.

And these little white stone houses are just silly, their white paint is perfect for reflecting the light and lighting up the road even more. This is not good. This is far, far from good.

If I was to kill someone now then I could almost certainly be seen, the guards would be summoned and I risk getting captured. This is not good at all!

The sound of the fishing ship unloading behind us is comforting as none of those creepy fishermen are chasing me, calling the guards or trying to flirt with me. That was why I talked to Coleman earlier, I was done with the fishermen flirting with me.

One of them even wanted me to sword fight with him. If you catch my drift.

And as for Coleman, I understand he is sad, depressed and a so-called failed leader but I wish you wouldn't worry so much about what I think of him. I know he wants to look strong for me, but I.. like him anyway.

If I wanted a cocky, strong man who would deal with whatever the world threw at him then I could have sex and love a noble man or one of the Overlord's puppet monarchs. But I don't want them. I want, I truly want Coleman (Not that I'll ever admit it to him, at least not yet).

But thankfully his cockiness gave me the excuse I needed to leave him and Abbic for a while, I wanted to explore the City myself and find an answer to why the Hunters can't come here. If I could find that out then maybe I could create a weapon, charm or something that would make them never want to find me.

A girl can hope!

The smell of sweet oranges, cake and honey filled my senses as we kept walking up the cobblestone road and I pulled my long black cloak and hood tightly and placed my hands on my swords.

I loved the cold feeling of their hilts.

"This is beautiful, don't ya think?" Abbic asked.

"I suppose it. It's a rubbish killing ground," I said coldly.

"Come on Assassin, there is some kind of romance here, isn't there?" Coleman said.

As much as I love his dark emerald eyes, fit body and movie star smile, I wasn't going to flirt with him in the open. That was never going to happen.

"Romance isn't what Assassins do. And where should I meet you both later?"

I heard something behind us but I couldn't subtly check yet.

"Ya not coming with us bud?" Abbic asked.

I smiled at her. "No. I have some exploring and investigating to do. But I'll be back in a few hours,"

We turned a corner and I saw Coleman look behind us, he shook his head at me. There were people behind us and Coleman clearly didn't want me to react but I wasn't good at doing what I was told.

"Okay Bud, look forward to ya returning to us,"

"Me too," I said to her.

The footsteps behind us were getting louder. Coleman looked at me, shaking his head.

I didn't listen.

I spun around.

There were five men.

Heavy.

Muscular.

Possibly armed.

Coleman dived for me.

I went to whip out my swords.

Coleman grabbed my hands.

He kissed me.

The five men simply walked past us, laughing, joking and enjoying their evening. They were simply five friends returning from a pub or something and I had almost attacked them, blowing our entire operation.

Coleman released his lips from mine and I realised I had completely forgotten that he was kissing me. Something I had longed for, for so long was now over, and I hadn't even tried to enjoy it.

Coleman walked away from me and his eyes were hollow like he was filled with the most disappointment he had ever felt. He probably thought I was going to enjoy it, savour it, want more. But I hadn't focused and he probably thought I was rejecting him completely.

I grabbed his hand but he shook me free and walked quickly over to Abbic and I just stood there.

Abbic looked at me but her and Coleman, my beautiful Coleman just kept walking on to complete their mission, like I was just another member of their Rebel team that was about to go on a solo mission.

Because in a way that was all I was now, just another Rebel, not Coleman's stunning love interest, I was just the woman who had shattered handsome Coleman's dreams of being with me.

I feared that I had just lost the only man that had ever loved me.

And that killed me inside.

CHAPTER 6
3 Days Left

As some strange kind of bells rang all over the City to mark the passing of the night and into a new day, Commander Coleman was furious at the Assassin. After everything they had been through together she didn't love him, like him or anything. She was simply manipulating him to get to her own goals.

No longer.

Coleman was never going to allow her back into the Rebellion, she was dead to him. How dare she not even pretend to respond to his kiss. He loved her. He wanted her. He gave her a chance when no one else would.

Damn her!

Coleman and Abbic went into a large wooden pub filled with rough wooden walls, plenty of drunk men and women and even a stray cat that hopped along the rows upon rows of tables.

There was something rather comforting about the normality of it all, Coleman would have imagined all their alcohol could have been sieged or destroyed by the Overlord, but here it all was accompanied with people who were happy, drunk and laughing with each other.

But Coleman didn't need a witch, wizard or warlock to know that these people were only drinking to mask their pain. It was the only bit of advice he had received as a young teenager in the City of Pleasure, *make sure you're drunk for when they come, it makes the Act a lot more bearable.*

Coleman had little doubt these people were doing the same.

The smell of urine, alcohol and grains filled Coleman's nose as he and Abbic went towards the massive bar on the far side of the pub. Coleman had to admit it was well stocked but the three barmen had already seen them and they didn't look happy.

Maybe it would have been a good idea to wear masks, cloaks or even hoods but Coleman wasn't going to look like the Assassin for anyone's love, money or respect. He was his own man, a great leader and he was here for a purpose.

Abbic marched over to the bar and sat up and smiled at a tall slightly muscular young barman who was carefully checking that the other barmen weren't within earshot.

The young barman's eyes were fixed on Abbic's long perfectly straight blond hair, and Coleman couldn't blame him. But as much as Coleman wanted this young man to be a friend, in this City he didn't have high hopes.

Coleman sat next to Abbic. "Two ales please,"

The barmen looked at Abbic and she shook her head.

The man went away.

"What was that about?" Coleman asked.

Abbic smiled. "Come on Bossie, I told tha man ya my husband, an alcoholic spiritualist,"

Coleman placed his face in his hands. "Really?"

"Ya, I had to give him something. We new, ya know? We need peeps to think we're normal,"

That wasn't the worse idea she had ever come up with, maybe the Assassin could have created something better… but he had to stop thinking like this. The Assassin was stunning, beautiful with her amazing body, black hair and eyes. But she was dead to him.

And that was final.

"Did ya say finding ya friend involved some code word?" Abbic said.

Coleman realised there was a reason why he always bought her along, he had completely forgotten about the so-called code word that the letters had told him about to find his friends in the City of Martyrs.

The only problem was the letters were sent years ago and maybe the sender was killed, exiled or simply left the City after the Overlord's grip tightened.

The young barman came over again. "Here you

go sir and beautiful Madame, our finest river water with a hint of lemon from the capital,"

Coleman smiled and nodded. "Tank you, do you know where one would find a *beautiful woman to be my guiding light to salvation?*"

He hoped he had the code right. He would seem pretty stupid without it.

The young barman shrugged and went away.

"What tha about?"

"That was the code. He doesn't know it. We need to ask around, try and find out if anyone here is a regular,"

Abbic leant forward. "Or ya just find out who owned the place when the letters were sent?"

Coleman shook his head. "Of course there is the simple option,"

Abbic finished her own river water and clicked the young barman back over.

"Yes Madame,"

Coleman could see if Abbic's eyes that she wanted to ask what time he got off shift so he could show her the sites and... that wouldn't be the worse idea. Maybe Coleman could encourage that.

Coleman leant closer to the man. "My friend is too shy to ask but what time do you get off shift?"

The barman smiled at Coleman. "Sorry but I don't swing that way and I'm more one on one,"

Coleman shook his head and smiled. Not exactly what he meant.

Abbic laughed hard. "Soz mate, he was asking

for me,"

The young barman stopped and went straight over to Abbic with a massive smile.

"I get off in a few minutes. My house isn't too far away?"

The entire house idea was interesting, if this man had a house to himself then maybe the barman could be recruited, trained and that could be their base of operations. It would be easier than trying to find the letter sender.

Abbic looked at Coleman. Coleman nodded.

"Um, ya that would be good," Abbic said clearly unsure of it all.

The barman smiled as he left to serve more people.

"What tha about Bossie?"

Coleman finished his river water, he wasn't keen on the strange sour taste it left on his tongue, but at least it was a good drink.

"You need to go with him. Convince him to join the Rebellion. Remember we need a base of operations,"

Abbic cocked her head. "Tha man hot though, what if he dies?"

Coleman threw his arms in the air. "He won't we'll protect him,"

The young barman went to Abbic wearing a long brown leather cloak that perfectly matched his dark brown eyes and smooth cheekbones, and Coleman supposed he understood why Abbic was attracted to him.

But Coleman still wanted his Assassin back, he wanted to run his fingers across her smooth skin, hair and body. He wanted her, needed her.

Yet the Assassin had made her choice.

Abbic wrapped her arm around the young barman's waist and they started to walk away.

The young barman stopped and turned towards Coleman. "Commander Coleman, I see you got my letters,"

CHAPTER 7
3 Days Left

I still wasn't impressed with myself for how I handled Coleman earlier. I did, do love him, he's great, funny and has everything I want in a man. But he thought I had rejected him. I had to prove him otherwise.

And what better way to prove I cared about him than to learn something critical about the City and its leader?

I knelt down on a flat slate rood overlooking a so-called grand entrance to a cathedral near the heart of the City. I wasn't impressed with its grand golden statues of gods know what, the jewels that encrusted it and even the little offering outside made by the other people.

It was silly how so many people would give away vital food, money and even body parts to an organisation like the Church that clearly didn't need it. The people inside this cathedral had to have millions of coins stacked neatly inside whilst there are people all throughout the Kingdom that barely had ten coins to their name.

It was disgraceful!

The smell of sweet oranges, overpriced perfumes and scented oils only added to my annoyance as I knelt here waiting for the leaders of the Cathedral to leave. There was no need to pump the air full of all these chemicals that quite frankly smelt wrong!

And the taste of mouldy oranges they left in my mouth was disgusting!

The sooner the City of Martyrs died the better.

The sound of soft voices came from below as I saw three figures in long white robes walk proudly out of the cathedral. I instantly didn't like that because they were all holding pots, boxes and clay containers full of coins and gold. They were probably taking it to their Masters, the bank or the most likely explanation as they were simply taking it home to add to their collections.

I had never understood why worshippers want to line the pockets of already-rich men. It wasn't going to make them rich in return, it wasn't going to gift them magical powers and it wasn't going to protect them.

But I couldn't help but feel like I had to do something to these men. These men were smiling, joking and mocking the poor souls that came here each day to worship and try to better their lives. That was wrong. These people had to understand that these so-called pointless peasants wanted their money to matter.

So perhaps I needed to help that money find its way back to more deserving owners.

I pulled my long black cloak and hood tightly over my body and face, and placed my hands on the cold hilts of my swords. These men were going to pay dearly.

"Did you see that pig face woman today?" the tallest man said.

"Ya with her pig face daughter. She gave me two hundred coins. I told her the Gods will need a lot more to transform her piggy little face," another one said.

I was so going to kill these so-called priests.

"I know! Those piggy people keep coming here. Giving us money. Long may they live!" the shortest man said.

"Long may they live and may they keep giving us their money!" another one said.

"Here, here!" they all shouted.

I had had enough.

I jumped down.

Whipping out my swords.

Slashed the throats of two men.

Blood spattering everywhere.

Blood painted the entrance.

Two corpses dropped.

I spun around.

Slicing off the hands of the tallest man.

Of course someone would have probably heard the banging, smashing and screams of the men and the gold, but I was hoping to be long gone before anyone came to check.

And the tens of candles that lit up this cobblestone street and cathedral entrance alone wasn't good. I had to be quick.

I pointed my swords at the man's chest and throat.

"I need information," I said coldly.

"You have failed Assassin. Your Father sees you here. He will come. He will kill you. You won't win,"

"How do you know about my father?"

"The Overlord is divine. He will lead us into the heavens so we shall all dine with the Gods and Goddesses at their diamond table,"

Wow! He was a real nutter.

"Why can't the hunters come here?" I asked.

The man smiled. "Because they are demons. Monsters. Witches. Wizards! They cannot step onto this holy ground. They will burn, die, slaughtered by its majesty,"

I was so going to take some gold for myself as a fee for listening to this nutter.

"Who controls the City?" I asked.

"The Gods and Goddesses rule here. The Overlord is a puppet to them. The Hand of Divinity rule on the Gods' behalf. They will smite you for your unholiness taint upon-"

I slit his throat.

I wasn't going to listen to his pointless words anymore. There were no gods, goddesses or any divine in the Kingdom. Sure there was magic from the witches, wizards and warlocks but they weren't pretending to rule in the name of False Gods.

Who ever the Hand of Divinity was, I had to find them, kill them and hopefully free the City in the process.

But first I had to make these corpses look a bit more... presentable.

So I went over to each corpse, sliced open their stomachs and heads and pulled out their guts, organs and brains for all to see and admire.

Of course almost no one would actually admire my work because they're all philistines, but I think my point would be clear enough.

I was here and I was ready to play.

CHAPTER 8
3 Days Left

Commander Coleman was livered with the Assassin, this is getting beyond a joke. This was outrageous!

Coleman stood on a long wooden balcony that overlooked thousands of little white houses with their hundred of thousands of candles lighting everything up. It was beautiful in a way but Coleman hated the large tide of torches walking through the streets.

He could taste the foul black smoke on his tongue as it filled his lungs. It was disgusting and all because presumably guards were walking around with torches looking for someone.

It had to be the Assassin.

It might have been pitch black but against the candles and burning torches of the guards, the City looked as if the sun was dimly rising.

Coleman didn't know how long they had before the Guards would knock on the young Barman's door, so they needed to be quick. All because of the Assassin. He might have once loved her but she was out of control, she was going to damn him, his friends and the Rebellion.

He couldn't allow that.

The sounds of muttering, wood creaking and torches burning made Coleman go back into the Barman's drawing room that had an impressive array of art on the walls with an immense black table in the middle surrounded by chairs.

It reminded Coleman of his war room back in the Rebellion's old headquarters but that was long gone.

Abbic and the Barman were kissing when Coleman went over to them and looked at the maps, documents and letters on the table in front of them. Then Coleman tapped on the table and they realised he was there.

"What are the torches in the streets? And who are you?" Coleman asked.

The Barman frowned. "There were whispers you carry an Assassin around. It seems they've killed someone and the guards are performing door to door searches,"

For Gods sake! This was not what Coleman needed.

"When the Guards search my house, I have somewhere for you to hide. I have alerted my friends to look for an Assassin and guide them here,"

Coleman stepped forward. "Who are you? Why

should we trust you?"

The Barman smiled. "Isn't that a question you should have asked earlier? You are in my house now,"

Coleman ignored him. "You're clearly no barman. No barman could ever afford this place,"

"Come on Bossie give tha man some slack," Abbic said.

"This art alone is worth a few hundred thousand," Coleman said gesturing to the stunning art on the walls.

"Fine. Your father knew my father. I met you once when our fathers met but you never looked at me,"

Coleman shrugged.

"My father was the Lord Castellan of this City," the Barman said. "My name should be Lord Castellan Richard of the House of Martyrdom,"

Coleman sunk to his knees as did Abbic at the sound of his name. The Lord Castellans were masterful people before the Overlord rose up 50 years ago. The people gifted that title were some of the kindness, most generous and master craftsmen in the Kingdom.

To hear of one alone was a rarity but to actually meet one in the flesh. Coleman had never met another soul who had been blessed by the presence of such a being.

But Coleman supposed the true reason why Lord Castellans were so graceful, respected and powerful were because they were apparently magic users in all but name. They were meant to be some of the most powerful witches, wizards and warlocks in the Kingdom, but Coleman didn't want to spoil this moment with the idea of magic.

"My Lord-" Coleman said.

Richard pointed at Coleman. "I do not have that title. My family ruled this City fairly, justly and everyone and I do mean everyone was happy here once. Now look at my City,"

"So ya wrote," Abbic said.

Richard nodded. "I did. My father died and I was… angry at the Overlord. I was hoping for aid but it never came,"

Coleman looked at the floor. "I… I am sorry,"

Richard placed a warm finger under Coleman's chin and raised it so Coleman looked into Richard's eyes.

"There will be time for sorrow but that time is not now. There are people to free, save and protect. That is our mission. I will tell you all I know but your friend is in great danger,"

"Let her rot," Coleman said, automatically.

Coleman heard a blade drop on the floor behind him.

"Is that how you feel about me?" the Assassin asked.

CHAPTER 9
3 Days Left

That bastard Coleman!

I had given him everything! I had fought for him! I was willing to die for him! And now he wants me to rot, die and leave him alone.

Well then maybe I should. Maybe I should just leave him. Let that stupid bunch of Rebels die. Let the Kingdom suffer.

Hell I might even join the Overlord and personally hunt down each and every Rebel til they are all dead!

Of course until Coleman, that annoying, sexy man with those deep emerald eyes, I can actually keep my emotions in check and I don't insulate every single bit of hope I have. Because whether he likes it or not he is stuck with me, as without me the Overlord will quickly and easily kill the Rebellion in one surgical strike.

And as for this drawing room, it is not the nicest

one I have seen. It's small filled with horrible tacky art that I suppose Coleman would find stunning, and even the black table in the middle. Come on, seriously?

A corpse would find a better table than that in a graveyard. I'm not even going to start on the chairs. All in all I am not impressed one bit.

I saw Coleman, Abbic and a rather hot barman staring at me, I just wanted to be human for a few seconds. Not a cold blooded, calculating assassin, just a woman who could love a man if she wanted.

I went over to Coleman and gestured that I wanted to hold his hands.

"Do you want me gone?" I asked, forcing some emotion into my voice.

"No," he said automatically.

"I didn't reject your kiss earlier. I honestly didn't realise it was happening. I was too focused on those… young men that could… that could have hurt you," I said, very proud of the emotion in my voice,

"You mean it?"

I nodded.

"Who is this woman?" the hot man asked with such arrogance I wanted to stab him right there and then.

"Richard, this is our Assassin. Assassin this is Richard, rightfully Lord Castellan of the House of Martyrdom,"

Now I know I was meant to act so surprised, shocked and in awe of this god amongst man, but seriously? This man wasn't going to beat me in a fight, he wasn't going to fight an army a thousand strong with a sword or do anything else that the stories apparently said he could do.

He was just a man. A hot but weak man at that.

"Ever fought before?" I asked.

Richard shook his head.

"Thought so. Your power might be in your blood. But it isn't activated until you rule the City, is it?" I asked.

"She's right," Richard said. "That's why I need your help,"

I pulled my long black cloak and hood slightly loose as I realised I had him exactly where I wanted him.

"You need us as much as we need you. Well, we don't need you too much, but the Rebellion will strike a deal," I said.

"What deal?"

Abbic wrapped her arms around him. "When we take ta City for ya, ya becoming an ally, give us a home, soldiers and food,"

Richard kissed Abbic and looked at me. "I agree but it can't happen. I have no idea how to take the City,"

And people honestly wonder why I worked alone for decades before I had to save the Rebellion, people are useless!

"What is the Hand of Divinity?" I asked.

Everyone looked blank at me. Typical.

"I killed three Priests-"

"You did not!" Richard shouted.

I gave him an evil smile.

"No wonder they're hunting you. Knocking down doors. Priests, Priestesses and all religious figures are seen as living Gods here. You don't kill them!"

I waved him silent. "Anyway the last one mentioned the City is ruled over by the Gods. But in reality the Hand of Divinity acts in their name,"

Still everyone looked at me blankly.

This was going well.

I heard something outside. It sounded like tens of voices walking up and down the street.

"I know somewhere we could find out. Your killing might be good for us actually," Richard said.

"How?" Coleman asked.

"Three Priests never get killed here so the Maiden of Light will call a summons in a few hours at nine O'clock. The last time a summons was called I was a boy and I remember seeing six people at the front,"

"Hands don't have six fingers, ya know?"

I smiled at Abbic. "They don't. But a hand has five fingers coming from a palm that is attached to the rest of the body, or in our case the rest of the Overlord's network,"

Oohs and aahs filled the drawing room as everyone else realised we had to go to that summons tomorrow (whatever a summons was!)

Someone thundered on the door.
They were smashing it down.
People were shouting outside.
"Quickly hide," Richard said.
The door shattered.
Guards poured in.

CHAPTER 10
2.75 Days Left

Commander Coleman hated being stuffed into a tiny wooden closet with the Assassin and Abbic next to him. Their weapons were jabbing into his back. Their hot breath was awful on the back of his neck.

He hated all of this.

The sound of the guards in their black armour made Coleman place his hand tightly on the hilt of his blade. If the enemy found them then he was going to fight, the enemy were not taking him and his friends alive.

That was a promise.

The disgusting smell of rot, sweat and death attacked Coleman's senses as the guards' footsteps got louder and louder and louder. Even Richard's voice was only a mutter compared to the heavy footsteps of the guards.

Richard could be trying to hint where the Rebels were hiding, but Coleman doubted it. He truly believed that Richard wanted their help.

The footsteps stopped in front of the closet.

Coleman prepared himself.

The closet door shattered.
Coleman stormed out.
Whipping out his sword.
The Guards were everywhere.
The Assassin jumped over him.
She attacked.
Coleman joined her.
His sword swung.
Shattering metal armour.
Slicing off heads.
Smashing bones.
Crunching arms.
The guards screamed.
They tried to fight.
Coleman and the Assassin didn't give them a take.
Abbic stabbed them.
She thrusted her knife into their chests.
Blood painted the walls.
Covered the art.
The floor flooded with blood.
The Guards screamed.
One tried to escape.
The Assassin rushed over.
Snapping his neck.
More Guards poured in.
They whacked the Assassin to one side.
They swarmed her.
Coleman dashed over.
Someone tackled him.
Slamming their fists into him.
Abbic grabbed the Guard's neck.
Snapping it off.
Coleman jumped up.

Raised his sword.

The Assassin was standing in a sea of corpses.

Richard ran over to them. Passing Coleman and Abbic cloaks.

They had to leave.

Coleman heard more guards coming.

Coleman realised the enemy knew they were here and that terrified him more than anything.

No backup. No support. Just four people against an army.

CHAPTER 11
2.75 Days Left

I barely managed to clean all the blood off my cloak but that's great fun. There is nothing like killing a bunch of foul ugly guards to get the heart pumping. I love it!

In my long black cloak and hood me, Richard, Coleman and Abbic went into a massive Cathedral filled with tens of thousands of sweaty, dirty poor people who attempted to wear their best for such an occasion, but in all honesty they were just wearing scraps of cloth.

I wanted to help them and I really hoped that the gold I gave to random houses helped some people, but I doubted they had kept it, probably gave it back to the Church for *safe keeping*.

Fools!

The Cathedral was rather beautiful with its massive gold domed roof that looked so perfect, so angelic and stunning in the way that it reflected the light from thousands of candles that floated in the air.

If anything I was stunned at the amazing scale of the Cathedral, I saw this earlier when we were coming into the docks and sure the golden dome was massive, but the Cathedral was immense. It easily went on for a good few miles in all directions. No wonder it could fit tens of thousands of people at any one time.

Actually I was even more surprised that we might have been a few hundred metres away from the main raised platform that surprise, surprise was solid gold and covered in jewels. But it wasn't packed. Everyone had some kind of personal space regardless of how many people were packed in here.

Behind me I heard some people in utter awe of the Cathedral's smooth dark blue walls with thousands of little images of saints, the Overlord and heroes painted in gold, jade and even bronze. The Overlord had really gone all out with this place with his Hand of Divinity and that was what I wanted to find out about.

The Hand had to be discovered but this wasn't a good killing ground. There were far too many people, it smelt and I was too far away from the raised platform where the Hand of Divinity would be. And as much as I wanted to stalk the crowd and edge closer to the target platform, there were still too many people.

"Look behind you," Coleman whispered.

I did and I was more than pleased to see there was an immense balcony built into the Cathedral covered in nothing except a golden star with rays of white light coming out of it in the centre. But I focused on the claw marks on the balcony around that star.

My thinking was someone important stood there so they could worship without any interference or having to deal with all these sweaty smelly people. I really wanted some of them to have a bath!

The entire cathedral went quiet as five people went up onto the raised platform and I checked behind me, and as I guessed there was a woman standing on the balcony.

But she troubled me. She was covered completely in thin sterile white armour, even her face was faceless with a thin plate of white armour covering it. She didn't look real at all, it was almost like she was beyond human and looking down at her mortal slaves.

"Turn around," Richard said firmly. "You'll draw attention,"

I turned my focus back on the five people on the raised platform. There was nothing too remarkable about three of them as they just wore plain black face masks made from iron and horrible long white robes. I couldn't imagine it would be too difficult to kill them but it all depended on what they had underneath.

Speaking of which I wouldn't mind seeing what Coleman had underneath.

"People of Martyrs!" a tall elegant woman said.

I hated her pompous voice as she sounded so arrogant, so superior to these people and she sounded like she was a Goddess.

"We are under attack," the woman said.

Everyone gasped in horror.

"It seems that there is a killer on the loose. They murdered in cold blood three of our most Holiest Priests. By attacking them. They attack our gods and you!"

I was expecting another gasp from everyone but only a quarter of the room gasped. Maybe these people weren't as religious as I believed. Maybe they did want their rulers dead after all.

"We tracked the killer down to the House of Former Lord Castellan Richard and I am sad to hear he is dead,"

Wow their information was awful.

"Now we will continue to hunt down the killer but our Honourable Maiden of Light would like to say a few words," the tall woman said, gesturing for everyone to turn around.

We did and I stared at the cold faceless mask of the woman on the balcony.

"My subjects. The Gods have spoken. You have all failed in your dedication. There were witnesses last night. None of you stepped forward to protect your Hand. So Hand judges you. Arrest a thousand people and the Gods will judge them,"

As the people at the very back of the Cathedral screamed in terror as the guards grabbed them, beat them and dragged them away. I focused on the coldness of her words. I couldn't imagine a human being so cold with such disregard for the life of others, but here this woman was.

Coleman grabbed my hand. I loved the sexy hot electricity that flowed between us but I squeezed it and released his hand.

"Richard, who is she?" I asked.

"The Maiden of Light is um… the true Ruler of the City. No one has ever seen her face but she is apparently the avatar of the Gods. They speak through her,"

"What happens if she dies?" I asked.

The Maiden just looked at me and I felt her borrowing into my mind.

I grabbed Coleman's arm. "We-"

"Rebels!" the Maiden shouted.

I hadn't even realised there were hundreds of guards lining the edges of the cathedral. They were storming towards us.

People screamed.

They ran.

They didn't care about their Hand.

The Hand flew off the raised platform.

They whipped out their white swords.

They were ready to fight.

So was I.

CHAPTER 12
2.66 Days Left

Commander Coleman was going to gut these bastards for daring to attack him and his friends.

He stood back to back with Richard and Abbic, each with their swords at the ready to chomp, slaughter and kill these guards and even the Hand.

The Hand with their black masks looked stupid anyway as they marched towards Coleman surrounded by the majesty and stunning beauty of the cathedral. Coleman loved the blue walls with their images of heroes.

Now it was his turn to be the hero.

The sounds of screaming, panic and pain filled the air as the tens of thousands of worshippers rushed out of the cathedral and some people fell and were crushed.

People were dying all because of the Maiden of Light.

She was staring at them and the Assassin was

staring at her.

"Kill her!" Coleman shouted.

The Assassin nodded and ran off into the crowd. Coleman had to protect her. Coleman couldn't let the Assassin face her alone there was something off about the Maiden.

Coleman raised his sword and prepared to attack.

The Guards flew at them.

Coleman swung his sword.

Sparks flew everywhere.

The Guards kept charging.

He felt Richard and Abbic press against his back.

They were being forced back.

Guards were everywhere.

The Guards swung their swords at Coleman.

He blocked.

Coleman screamed as the force of the impact whacked his sword away.

He didn't have a weapon.

He had to break formation.

Everyone broke it as one.

They all rolled away.

The Guards swung.

They missed.

They slashed their own chests.

Coleman kept rolling.

He grabbed his sword.

Jumped up.

Thrusted it into someone's chest.

The Guards kept coming.

Coleman needed a new plan.

They were outnumbered.

Abbic was being overwhelmed.

Coleman couldn't let her die.

He dashed over.

Ramming his sword into a Guards' back.

Then all the Guards simply took a few steps back and Coleman felt his stomach churn as he saw the three members of the Hand of Divinity with their black iron masks hold their swords at Coleman's, Abbic's and Richard's chest.

Coleman wanted to attack them all now but he noticed a strange white energy crackling around them. He didn't know what weapons they were holding but nothing good was ever going to happen by attacking them head on.

He needed a new plan.

"You dare attack the Maiden," someone said but it was clearly a man.

"What it to ya?" Abbic asked. "We gonna gut ya all,"

One of the Hand swung their sword in the air and Abbic screamed in crippling pain as white crackling energy wrapped around her.

"Stop that!" Coleman shouted.

Another of the Hand gestured they would do the same to Coleman.

"You can't do this. Our friend will find you and kill you," Coleman said.

The three members of the Hand exchanged

looks with each other and made a series of clicks. Coleman wished the Assassin had taught him the clicking language like she had offered because it sure would have been useful about now.

"You will not do that to us!" Richard shouted, clearly knowing the language.

One of them swung their sword in the air and the white energy crackled around Richard.

"We will imprison, kill you and send a direct message to the Assassin. Her father wants her back,"

Coleman wanted to explain how that message would only end in their deaths but he just stayed silent. Nothing good was going to happen if he spoke. He fully planned on just leaving these deluded Holy figures to their delusions that would certainly come back to kill them in the end.

"Commander Coleman, I trust we will not have any problems with you," another asked gesturing that they would swing their sword.

"Of course not, *my Lords and Ladies*," Coleman said, mockingly but seriously enough.

The woman in the long white robes who spoke to the masses earlier stepped forward.

"Good, Guards take him and the other two away," the woman said before she looked at the three in the masks. "You three, kill the Assassin. Kill her,"

Coleman's stomach churned and churned and churned as he forced himself not to lash out. He had to be taken away and not end up like Abbic and Richard, who were still screaming, if he was free to move about then maybe he could help her in the long term.

But now he was captured Coleman had a very bad feeling about the mission.

Especially with the entire remains of the Rebellion coming here in a few days.

CHAPTER 13
2.5 Days Left

I hated this Maiden of Light for daring to kill me and my friends. Who the hell does she think she is? No one and I mean no one attacks us and gets to live! This is beyond outrageous!

I pulled my long black cloak and hood tightly over myself as I stepped onto the horrible massive stone balcony where the Maiden of Light was when I last saw her. I hated everything about this balcony from its foul blue walls to utterly arrogant scripture saying how amazing she was.

I wasn't to gut her.

Even the horrid smell of burning incense was nothing to make me furious at her, and the sounds of my friends in trouble made me want to burn this entire Cathedral to the ground…

Oh. Now that's an idea!

The sound of three heavy footsteps came from behind me and when I looked at them I was hardly surprised to see the three members of the Hands with their black iron masks. Two men, one woman.

They all had their long white swords with magical energy crackling around them. I knew what they did but I hoped they wouldn't affect me.

They all swung their swords in the air.

The magic energy crackled around me.

It was closing in.

I wasn't scared.

I wanted the pain.

I wanted to feel.

I wanted to kill the magic.

The magic energy diffused away from me. Coward!

With the three iron mask wearers exchanging glances with each other, I took my chance.

I flew at them.

Jumping into the air.

Whipping out my swords.

I landed on one of their necks.

I pulled my momentum to throw the Hand Member to the ground.

Ramming my swords into his head.

The other two swung at me.

I ducked.

They lost their balance.

I kicked one.

The woman grabbed my head.

I backflipped.

Making her fall.

I stomped on her face.
Something cracked.
She didn't die.
The last man charged at me.
I jumped.
Not in time.
He caught me.
Ramming me into the stone of the balcony.
It started cracking.
I went to scream.
I looked below.
One of my friends might help me.
They were gone.
They were in danger.
They could be dead.
The man grabbed my throat.
He squeezed.
My friends were in danger!
I kicked him in-between the legs.
He fell to the ground.
He moaned.
I stomped on his manly goods.
He screamed.
I whacked his head.
I kicked him again and again.
His blood splattered everywhere.
He tried to stand up.
I grabbed the mask.
Ripping it off.
It was melted into his face.

I threw the mask at the woman.

She ducked.

She wasn't attacking me.

I jumped on the barely living man.

Grabbing his head.

I smashed his head on the floor.

Over and over.

And over.

All until there was nothing left in my hands and there was only the shattered corpse of a man in front of me.

I stood up and stared at the woman who was impressively holding a shaky sword at me like she would actually kill me. I always admire ambition so I had to give her her due.

But my friends were in danger and I don't stop for anyone when that happens.

So I simply walked to her, gently took the sword of her hand and wrapped my hands around her throat.

"Where are my friends?" I asked coldly.

The woman didn't answer so I snapped her neck.

I went over to the spot on the balcony where the Maiden of Light stood each service and I understood why she stood here. It felt as if this spot had power, purpose and the admiration of hundreds of thousands locked into the very stone. Which was off considering there were no markings on the stone ground.

Yet as beautiful as this all looked it was a symbol of the Overlord's power, influence and corruption in the City so it had to be annihilated.

    I just didn't know how but I would find a way.

    Just like I always do.

CHAPTER 14
2.25 Days Left

Commander Coleman sat in a large metal cage with Abbic and Richard hissing, screaming and moaning as the white energy crackling them kept torturing them.

Coleman felt the cold metal cage vibrate and bang as it was pulled through the streets of the City of Martyrs with its little white houses and the thousands of candles lighting the way.

It was strange that there were so many candles lit even though it was only early evening with the sun brightly lighting the evening sky, Coleman had bigger problems so he didn't care too much about the ways of the City.

He had to figure out a way to escape, the guards had escorted him, Abbic and Richard to various cells, transports and now they were meant to be taking them to some advanced interrogation centre, but Coleman wasn't going to let that happen.

The sounds of pain from his friends grew more intense and Coleman hoped the so-called Maiden of Light was going to get an agonising death. She was in charge. She gave the orders. It was her that was going to die.

Pulling the metal cage along were two large black horses and one of the Hand were guiding them. Coleman wished he could reach that idiot Hand driving the cage and kill them but he couldn't reach.

From what he could see of the Hand member, it wasn't the tall woman with white robes that spoke to the masses nor was it the three members with their black iron masks. It looked to be a man wearing long white robes with red crosses and golden jewellery covering the robes.

It was clear that he was important so Coleman hoped he wasn't that good at combat.

The sound of people singing, chanting and shouting came from ahead and Coleman raised his head to see a massive mob of people with knives, pitchforks and spades standing there.

They blocked the street completely.

The metal cage came to a stop and Coleman went over to the cage's door at the back and inspected it. He had hoped for screws or something easy to break open.

But the door disappeared.

"Move!" the Hand Member said. "I am Lord Bishop Anchor, I demand you to move!"

No one moved. Everyone smiled.

"What say you Rebels?" the man at the very front of the mob said.

Coleman stood up. "I say we can help each other,"

The mob nodded. "What say you Commander, can you free us?"

"Yes," Coleman said.

"What say you Lord Bishop, do you want to live?"

"Ha! You cannot hurt me. I am-"

The mob flew forward.

They raised their pitchforks.

They raised their spirits.

They raised everything.

The Lord Bishop whipped out his sword.

Magical energy crackled around them.

Coleman shook Abbic.

She hissed louder.

He had to help.

The mob started screaming.

Abbic moved her arms.

Coleman realised something. The more the mob screamed. The freer Abbic was.

Coleman shook her head more and more.

The Lord Bishop screamed.

The mob were stabbing him with their pitchforks, spades and knives.

The Lord Bishop screamed.

Then all went silent.

The man who presumably led the mob walked up

to the metal cage, and Coleman had a good long look at him. He was clearly a skilled worker with his smoother-than-most hands and his well maintained features. But there was something strange about him, he didn't seem bothered that he had just killed a member of the Hand of Divinity, he must have known the consequences. The man didn't seem bothered.

To Coleman that normally meant one of two things. One, the man was somewhere on the crazy scale, or two, he had killed so many times it didn't affect him more.

Coleman didn't know what one he hoped for.

"Grab his sword," Coleman said.

The man clicked his fingers and the Lord Bishop's sword flew over to him. He passed it to Coleman.

He had no idea how it worked but it was clearly some kind of magic, and normally magic worked by a power, a focus and an effect. Coleman hoped he was right about the focus being the sword and the effect (he really hoped) would be the unlocking of the cage and freeing of his friends.

The power? He had no clue but it could be something as simple as his Will.

Coleman closed his eyes and imagined Abbic and Richard being free from the magical energy that trapped him. He swung the sword.

Nothing happened.

Coleman focused on the love, respect and

admiration he had for them. He didn't want them trapped, he wanted them free to live, love and fight against the Overlord. He swung the sword again.

Nothing.

Coleman swore as he tried a final time. This time Coleman really, really focused on his feelings for both Abbic and Richard, then he focused extremely hard on imagining them being free.

Two bodies hit the ground.

Coleman opened his eyes and went over to them both, he helped them up and gave Abbic a massive hug and Richard a hard handshake.

The mob clapped.

"Impressive Commander. Not seen that for decades," the Mob Leader said.

Horns, marching and flames roaring echoed around the street as everyone saw a stream of black armoured guards marching from the Cathedral down to them. Coleman had to be quick.

He went to the "walls" of the metal cage, closed his eyes and focused. He wanted to slaughter the cage, destroyed it and most importantly be free.

He swung the sword.

The metal cage turned to ash.

Arrows pounded the ground.

Guards fired.

Guards charged at them.

The mob fled.

Coleman grabbed Abbic and Richard.

Dragging them away.

They were free and ready to bring the Maiden of Light's rule crashing down!

CHAPTER 15
2 Days Left

Something I absolutely love about the religious folks of the world is their ability to find the most amazing places to hide their alcohol. It has taken me over three hours, a lot of killing and sighting for me to finally find enough alcohol to blow this Cathedral up.

I couldn't help but smile at my impressive pile of hundreds of wine, brandy and ale bottles and even more crates of Gods know what alcohol that was all piled perfectly in the middle of the Cathedral.

Blowing this place up was definitely going to be a highlight of my life. Getting rid of those horrible blue walls with their silly images, blowing up that stupid balcony and turning this symbol of my father's corruption, power and influence to ash.

That was going to make me extremely happy.

Sure I really, really wanted my beautiful Coleman to be here with me, I would love to stare into his stunning dark emerald eyes in the dancing light of the flame, but I sadly had to do this alone.

I do love burning things down though.

But all the alcohol made the cathedral sink of wine, bad ale and sick. I was starting to question if everything in that pile was alcohol.

Loosening my long black cloak and hood, I held out my flaming torch and prepared to throw it at the pile. Sure it would take a few seconds to light, blow and burn but I'll be lying if I said I wasn't concerned.

Two arrows shot at me.

I threw the torch at the pile.

More arrows fired.

It knocked the torch off course.

It landed far away from the pile.

I spun around.

Instantly raising my arms as the Maiden of Light with her horrid white faceless mask and white robes walked towards me with four guards carrying crossbows.

"I admit your arrival was a surprise, Jasper," the Maiden of Light said.

How the hell did she know my true name? Besides my dickhead of a father only Coleman knows it and I doubted either of them would tell her my name.

"It was fun watching you run about like the little mortal fool you are," she said.

I watched the guards walk around me. I couldn't let them near that flaming torch.

"What is your aim here Jasper? You cannot win. The Gods and Goddesses have foreseen your death here,"

I have never quite understood why people use that as a fear tactic. I have never feared death and now... now I actually think I am living a life worth living and I have a purpose.

And right now that meant my purpose was destroying the Hand of Divinity, including her.

I whipped out my two swords.

"Oh Jasper, I was hoping we could have avoided all this. Your Father will be most disappointed,"

She waved a hand and the torch went out.

Rage filled me.

I flew at her.

I swung.

She ducked.

She whipped out her own swords.

We clashed.

Sparkes flew.

Sparkes flew!

I kicked her.

She dodged.

She punched me.

Throwing me across the cathedral.

I slammed into a wall.

She disappeared.

She punched me from behind.

Throwing me forward.

She kicked me.

I jumped up.
Swinging my swords.
We clashed.
I punched.
I kicked.
I headbutted.
She dodged them all.
Our swords clashed against.
I pressed all my weight on her.
She jumped away.
I fell forward.
She rammed her swords into my back.
I screamed.
I wasn't dead yet!
I rolled over.
Raised my swords.
She bought her swords down.
We clashed.
Sparkes flew everywhere.
Whooshing filled the cathedral.

And I could never not smile as I watched her eyes widen in utter horror as she realised I had made her fight in such a way that she would be closer to the pile of alcohol.

She kicked me in the stomach as we both watched the massive pile of alcohol light up and become a flaming inferno.

The Maiden of Light and her guards simply walked away.

I tried to stand up but I couldn't. My back was

hurting too much. I felt blood run down my back.

I couldn't escape. I was going to die here.

More and more alcohol started to light up. It wouldn't be long until the bottles exploded.

My swords started to heat up and I knew what I had to do.

I rolled over and rammed my swords into the alcohol fuelled flames. Then I forced myself to sit down and took off my long black cloak and my leather armour beneath.

Exposing my bare bleeding flesh.

My swords were starting to glow now.

I took out the red hot swords and pressed them against my wounds.

I screamed in agony.

Crippling plain filled me.

But my wounds were healed.

A bottle exploded.

Splashing flaming alcohol everywhere.

Adrenaline flooded me.

More bottles exploded.

I jumped up.

And ran.

More bottles exploded.

The entire cathedral burnt.

Toxic smoke filled the Cathedral.

I kept running.

A deafening whoosh came from behind.

I saw the door outside.

I ran as fast as I could.

I jumped through the door.

The explosion rushed past me.

My ears rang.

But my eyes focused on the twenty guards aiming their crossbows at me.

CHAPTER 16
2 Days Left

Commander Coleman sat with Abbic and Richard at a massive oak table inside a wonderfully dark room with tens, maybe even hundreds of peasants around the table, waiting for their leader to return.

Besides from the honestly horrible smell of sweat, dirt and urine coming from the peasants, Coleman loved the atmosphere at it felt as if everyone was here illegally and this was all one big conspiracy against the Rulers of the City of Martyrs.

Coleman had to convince them to fight, kill and slaughter the enemy and hopefully make sure they wanted to join the Rebellion. He wasn't sure who these people were but after travelling around with them for six hours now, he was at least fairly sure he could trust them. But the sounds of their talking, muttering and laughing didn't exactly comfort Coleman.

At the very end of the table a large old man sat down wearing a dirty cloth, a belt and a sword at his waist. Out of everyone he had seen, this was the first person who screamed leader to Coleman.

The man just stared at them for a few moments before he waved his friends away and everyone took a few steps back.

"Ya father would be eased Commander," the man said.

Coleman leant forward. "You knew my father?"

"Yea, we were once rebels like yourself us lot. Your father sent us here to die, become a distant memory and let me run *his* Rebellion as he wished,"

There were plenty of rumours about the Rebellion's twisted history that Coleman had heard of over the years, including something about a legion of troublemakers sent to a forgotten City to fight, kill and hopefully die themselves.

"You kept fighting all this time?" Coleman asked.

Richard placed a gentle hand on Coleman's arm.

"What my friend means-"

"We know what he means. He didn't keep fighting. We failed. We ran away and didn't die here like we were meanna," the man said.

Coleman stood up. "My father might of had his reasons. But I am not my father, the Rebellion needs you again,"

All Coleman could hope for at that moment was not to get attacked, sworn at or reported to the Overlord's puppets.

The man stood up too. "My name is Justicus Pilon… but my friends call me Justin,"

Justin bowed to Coleman as did every single man and woman under his command.

"Tonight we do not fight for the Rebellion, the people who hated us. Tonight we fight for Coleman, for blood and for Freedom," Justin said.

Everyone cheered.

"And when we claim this City, you will have your freedom," Coleman said.

Justin smiled.

"Then everyone, prepare ya weapons, ya food and ya loved ones. We march on the City at dawn,"

Everyone walked away so only Justin, Abbic and Richard were in the room with Coleman.

Justin walked over to them.

"What ya mean boyo marching at dawn?" Abbic asked.

"Ya didn't tell 'em did ya?" Justin said to Richard.

Coleman frowned at Richard. "What aren't you telling us *Lord Castellan*?"

"The Cathedral might have burned but that isn't the Hand's main base of operations," Richard said.

That was ridiculous, how the hell was Coleman meant to lead, make a plan and defeat the enemy if everyone was only telling him half the information!

"Where is ta Assassin?"

Coleman felt his body warm and sweat roll down his back as he realised that his beautiful Assassin was missing. She had destroyed the main cathedral hours ago and now it was completely ash.

That alone would trouble him but she always found him somehow and she hasn't yet. That wasn't like her.

Coleman wanted to shout, scream and demand some kind of search party or form some kind of plan to save her, but he had no idea where to look.

He had to save her by any means.

"Where is their main base then?" Coleman asked firmly.

Richard exchanged glances with Justin. "There's a temple underground. Simple layout. Simple defences. Simple to attack. But the Maiden defends it herself. Going inside is a death sentence,"

Coleman laughed. "Oh Richard, Justin, you clearly have no idea what lengths I'll go to to rescue the Assassin. We need her,"

Justin slammed his fist on the table. "Or do *ya* need her?"

Coleman said nothing.

"I will not send my forces back for ya to rescue ya girl," Justin said walking away.

Coleman looked at Richard and Abbic. "I will save her,"

Abbic jumped off her chair and smiled. "Course ya will, I gonna help ya too Bossie. Assassin my friend and friends protect each other,"

Both Coleman and Abbic looked at Richard. He rolled his eyes.

"Fine, I'll help you save your Assassin,"

CHAPTER 17
1 Day Left

I was not happy!

These idiot guards dared to capture me, lock me up and dump me in some fucking cell! The cheek!

I can promise them that the second I get out of this cell I am going to gut them so much that the Overlord can see their mutilated corpses from his palace!

I honestly wouldn't mind being trapped in a wet dirty box room made of horrible stone, but the smell is awful. Some overweight prisoner must have taken an almighty poo in the corner and the guards haven't cleared it up yet.

Even the coldness of the cell isn't making me any happier, I love the cold of metal bars but as I ran my fingers across them icy coldness isn't shot into me. It was a pathetic kind of coldness.

I had had enough! I was getting out of here!

Of course the idiot guards hadn't given me any

weapons and it was only because I snapped a neck of a guard that I had been allowed to keep my long black cloak and hood. Thankfully I always keep a small blade in there.

I slipped it out of a pocket but judging by the bar metals and tough stone walls I wasn't going to be able to escape that way, but on second thought I could have sworn these stone walls were made of flint.

And flint can light.

Granted I honestly can't remember the last time I lit poo up, but I know it burns well and guards don't like fires. Especially when the Maiden of Light gives them specific orders to keep me alive whilst she arranges transport to the Capital (and my dick of a father) for me.

I went over to one of the flint walls, chipped away at it and managed to break off a piece of flint.

Then I looked at the massive pile of poo and realised I had to do the most disgusting job in my assassin career, I had to move it around the cell. Believe me, this sounds unneeded and I wished it was, but if I just lit up a pile in the corner then the guards wouldn't care.

I needed to make them care.

I went over to the pile (and really held my breath) as I gently kicked it to different areas in the cell, giving me six perfectly small piles of poos.

I lit each one up.

Black smoke filled the cell and filtered into the stone corridor beyond where I hoped the guards.

Then the piles started popping.

Little fires started elsewhere.

The fire spread.

I pressed my back against the metal bars. I didn't want a raging fire. The flames consumed the rest of the cell.

The flint started exploding.

Shit!

I pulled my hood over my face. Shards of flint hit me. Slicing my cloak.

The Guards shouted.

They ran towards me.

The flames got closer.

They licked my flesh.

I felt hands grab me.

Massive shards of flint exploded.

Deadly shards flew towards us.

I jumped back.

The guards screamed.

Their blood ran down their faces.

They were crying on the ground.

More flint exploded.

Shredding them to pieces.

And there I had it, I snapped the neck of one guard, took his weapons and simply left the exploding flint to do my job for me.

Now I was free, armed and more than ready to kill every single enemy in this place.

CHAPTER 18
1 Day Left

Commander Coleman stood with his sword drawn as he peeked around a corner of a little white house and looked at a heavily guarded cobblestone street.

Abbic and Richard were behind Coleman and everyone was ready to move. There was a small manhole cover in the middle of the street that was the entrance to the underground temple dedicated to the Maiden of Light.

And that was where his Assassin was.

Coleman had to save her, he loved her, he wasn't going to let her die. But there were so many silly guards here that needed to die.

It was annoying as hell that the exiled Rebels had abandoned Coleman, but he didn't need them. He was a leader and an amazing fighter and he was going to do whatever it took to save the woman he loved.

Richard had tried to warn him earlier about the

maze the temple was and how it could take them hours just to enter the main temple complex, but Coleman did not care. This was the Assassin he was going to save.

Coleman looked at Abbic and Richard were climbing on the white rooftops of the houses, they nodded at him. They were ready.

Coleman raised his swords.

He charged.

The guards didn't see him.

Coleman jumped on them.

Ramming his sword into their chests.

Ribs cracked.

Blood flooded on the ground.

Coleman hacked his way through them.

Armour smashed.

Bones shattered.

Coleman stomped on their skulls.

The Guards knew he was there.

They charged at him.

They swung.

Coleman ducked.

They all kicked him.

Coleman felt the impacts.

He hissed.

Pain flooded through him.

He wasn't stopping.

Coleman ran.

Jumping into the air.

He swirled his swords.

Becoming a hurricane of death.

The guards tried to block him.

They couldn't.

Coleman's swords ripped into their armour.

Slicing into their warm flesh.

Abbic and Richard jumped down.

Thrusting their swords into the Guards.

It was a slaughter.

And within a few minutes Coleman, Abbic and Richard had massacred all the guards, but the problem with these sorts of places where there were always more guards just round the corner, Coleman had to be quick.

They all went over to the manhole cover that was nothing more than a little black iron circle in the ground, but Coleman instantly spotted a problem.

It was magically sealed.

"Anyone know how to break a magic seal?" Coleman asked.

Abbic shrugged, so did Richard.

Coleman pointed a finger at Richard. "Wait a minute, you're a Lord Castellan. You can break it,"

Richard frowned. "I am not a Lord Castellan yet,"

Coleman stood up. "Maybe you don't need to rule to be a Lord Castellan. The power is in your blood. You just need to believe in yourself,"

Coleman had no idea if it was true but they didn't have a lot of other options at this point.

"Don't be-" Richard said.

"Don't ya dare call my Bossie silly. Ya need to take responsibility for life!"

Richard stared at Coleman. "I don't know how to be a Lord Castellan,"

The sound of guards from streets away made Coleman's stomach tense.

"Say it with me, *you are a Lord Castellan. You are powerful. You are a Leader. You are magical*,"

Richard repeated it but he didn't sound convinced.

"For Gods and Goddesses sake, Richard focus. You are a born leader. You secretly fought against the Overlord for years. You survived. I saw your schemes in your house. You funded, supported and loved those exiled Rebels," Coleman said.

Richard nodded.

"You have an amazing mind. You are willing to die to save someone you hardly know. That makes you a born leader to me. And Leaders are what Lord Castellans are!"

Richard smiled. "I am Lord Castellan,"

It was really starting to annoy Coleman that he wasn't saying it convincingly enough.

The guards were getting closer.

Coleman grabbed Richard's arm. "Who are you?"

Richard looked to the ground but Coleman grabbed his face and made him look him in the eye.

"Who are you!" Coleman shouted.

"I am Lord Castellan Richard of the House of the Martyrdom and I demand you to release me!"

The air crackled with magical energy as Coleman released him and the very air hummed, popped and banged as something was happening.

Richard was engulfed in bright white fire but he did not scream. He laughed, smiled and wanted this to happen.

Coleman watched the lightning shoot around them all as Richard presumably became and took up his birthright.

When the white fire got absorbed into Richard, he fell to his knees and Coleman noticed that Richard was stronger, tougher and every single part of him had changed slightly. His skin was thick, his jawline stronger and his hair thicker.

Coleman realised he was looking at the peak of human attractiveness and physique. (He just hoped the Assassin still had eyes for him after this battle)

"Guards! Flamethrowers!" Abbic shouted.

Coleman just looked at Richard.

Richard went over to the manhole cover.

He extended his arms.

Flamethrowers screamed through the air.

Coleman grabbed Abbic.

He pulled her to safety.

They rushed over to Richard.

The air crackled.

The manhole exploded into shards.

Richard threw the shards of the guards.

All three of them jumped down into the temple below and Coleman was ready to save the woman he loved and kill anyone who tried to stop him.

CHAPTER 19
0.75 Days left

Whoever created this stupid underground temple was going to die!

It was ridiculous that I had just spent six hours (including a quick power nap) searching, running and killing my way through its twisted network of horrible black stone tunnels.

I had had enough and I was going to find the Maiden of Light and slaughter her for ever trapping me here in the first place!

Raising my swords as I went along another awful stone tunnel, I prepared myself for whatever horror or silly guard was going to try and stop me.

But to my surprise, I saw a large door ahead of me made from solid gold with tens of candles lighting it up. Someone clearly wanted any onlookers to see its amazingly smooth golden surface, sparkling jewels and even the little pieces of scripture in the door that praised the Gods and Goddesses.

It was clear who was behind there and a wave of pure excitement filled me as I relaxed my body, loosened my shoulders and prepared to storm in there and kill the Maiden of Light.

She had to be in there.

But I felt my stomach tighten, relax then tighten again as I realised that I was alone down here. My beautiful Coleman wasn't here to protect (and fail) me, he wasn't here to jump in front of a sword or try to die for me. Like I found that attractive anyway (I didn't).

If I went into that room then I was truly alone, no one would be there to support me, protect me or do anything. If I got into trouble then I was dead.

I kept walking towards the massive golden door, all I had ever wanted from life was to live a life beyond killing, I wanted a life worth living. And Coleman had given me that, if I died today then I would have died sacrificing myself for something greater than I ever could have imagined.

I was going to die so millions of people could have a shot at freedom.

As I walked past the tens of candles they started to go out one by one, then two by two and they all went out and I was alone in the darkness.

The freezing cold darkness surrounded me and I couldn't tell where the stone tunnel walls began and my body ended. It was pitch dark.

Then the golden door started glowing. First it was bright gold, then red, then white, and with each colour change I realised my long leather cloak and hood were getting hotter and hotter and hotter.

Shoot!

I ran away as quickly I could before the door exploded. Sending me flying.

Boiling hot gold splashed all over the tunnel and a tiny amount splashed against my long black cloak.

I forced myself back up and to my utter amazement that arrogant Maiden of Light with her long white robes and white faceless mask was just standing there where the door once was.

The dark stone walls of the tunnel were now covered in bright shiny gold allowing me to see everything because of the horrible white light the Maiden was projecting.

Of course she didn't have any facial expression but I could have sworn I felt her smiling or just curious about what I would do next. I wanted to run, fight and kill her, but I felt like that was what she wanted. I supposed she had to wait to find out.

Fat chance!

I charged at her.

She flicked her hand and I froze. I really, really hate witches!

"Relax now Jasper. My spell will wear off in a few moments. But we have time my darling,"

I wanted to rip her throat out for saying that.

"Do not struggle my darling Jasper, your mother made me promise never to hurt you but I never did like her. The Overlord was a fool for choosing her,"

My eyes narrowed. "What do you know about my mother?"

"Jasper, you and your brother, were failures as far as the Overlord was concerned. Deficit stock from a defected woman,"

I forced myself not to scream or lash out. I had to keep her talking but I would end her painfully for mentioning my brother as deficit. The Overlord never should have killed him.

"So that is why Jasper, The Overlord moved onto more correct women with your mother's weaknesses, problems and… well, abnormalities,"

I felt my fingers move and the Maiden stared at me.

"We can fight in a moment and I will kill you, but I think I have time to answer one more question on your behalf,"

I rolled my eyes and noticed my swords were on the ground a few metres from me. When it was time I had to be quick.

"Your father had so many women lined up to bed. So many women to give him rightfully children but he chose your mother. A weak, pathetic abnormal woman and look where that got him. So that is why I came to the City of Martyrs,"

I laughed hard. "Seriously? You ruled over the City just because you were heartbroken. Just because the tyrant you loved, didn't choose you?"

The Maiden shook her head. "You silly little girl. I was never heartbroken. Who did you think birthed the Hunters?"

My eyes widened.

The Maiden flew at me.
The final battle begins now!

CHAPTER 20
0.75 Days left

Commander Coleman was fuming at this Gods forsaken place, who would create such a pointless maze of dark stone tunnels? It was silly, pointless and Coleman was going to kill all the Guards that dared to stop him getting to the woman he loved.

Coleman slashed the throat of another guard as the corpse fell onto the cold stone tunnel floor. He looked around seeing Abbic and Richard standing their swords drawn.

They were all ready to act, kill and protect Coleman. But he needed a direction, he needed something to tell him where his beautiful Assassin was.

Heavy footsteps ran towards them.

Coleman spun.

More horrible black armoured guards charged at them.

Coleman raised his sword.

More and more guards were coming.

Far too many for them to kill.

Coleman didn't care. He was going to fight. He was going to kill for what he believed in.

Richard flew forward.

Magical energy crackling around him.

Coleman joined him.

Both him and Abbic charged.

Roaring as loud as they could.

Richard shot out his hand.

Magical pink lightning shot out.

Disorienting the guards.

Coleman swung his sword.

Hacking the guards to death.

The guards recovered.

They ran at Coleman.

Swinging their swords.

Firing their crossbows.

Firing their arrows.

Richard thrusted out his hands.

Magical energy crackled.

It hissed, popped and exploded.

Richard screamed.

His hands burnt.

Coleman smashed the head of a guard into a wall.

Richard was out.

He was useless.

Coleman dashed over to him.

The guards kept coming.

Hints of smoke filled the tunnel. Coleman hated

the smell.

Abbie shrieked.

She was thrown against a wall.

She fell to the ground.

The Guards raised their swords.

Coleman rushed over there.

Hands grabbed him.

Forcing him to the ground.

The cold steel of a sword kissed his neck and Coleman stopped moving, struggling and trying to escape as he realised that the guards were holding him too tight.

"Stop," a young female voice echoed around the tunnel.

Whilst Coleman had heard more than enough voices in his time, he would never forget the voice of the Maiden of Light. Especially as she walked past her guards with her wonderful white robes and interesting faceless mask.

But Coleman couldn't understand why she appeared ghostly, none of her looked solid or of this world.

"Commander, I must admit I would have loved to have seen you die in person. But alas I am killing your Assassin, this is the day the Rebellion dies truly,"

Coleman felt rage fill him. This Maiden of false gods and goddesses was attacking his stunning Assassin. He wasn't having any of that!

"Kill the girl," the Maiden ordered.

The entire tunnel lit up.

Flames rushed down the tunnel.

The guards loosened their grip.

Coleman ducked.

Flames roared through the tunnel.

Coleman felt his body warm.

Sweat dripped down his face.

When the flames were gone and Coleman stood up, flaming, smouldering corpses were all around him. Richard and Abbic stood up with their eyes wide in confusion.

Coleman couldn't blame them. The entire tunnel had just been attacked with some kind of flame weapon. Yet he and his friends had survived.

And there was only one group of people he knew that would try to save them.

"Turns out ma peeps like ya?" Justin said as he walked down the tunnel holding some kind of flamer weapon.

But what impressed Coleman ever more was the massive long line of exiled Rebels behind Justin that looked like they wanted a fight.

Justin knelt.

All the exiled Rebels knelt to Coleman.

"Well Commander, ya wanted us to fight. We're ya army,"

Coleman smiled. "Get-"

Deafening chances of blood, murder and slaughter echoed around the tunnel from behind Coleman.

He saw little flickering torches. There were

hundreds. The Maiden of Light appeared in front of Coleman.

"Enjoy every single last one of my Guard," she said.

Coleman thrusted his sword through the ghostly woman and to his surprise tears formed in her eyes and she bleed.

Then disappeared.

Justin grabbed Coleman.

"Go! Find ya woman. We'll hold 'em back!"

Justin and the Exiled Rebels pushed past Coleman. They wanted to fight. They wanted Coleman to succeed.

Abbic grabbed him. "Bossie, ya know we lost without her. Get her back,"

Coleman was never going to argue with his closest friend. He had to go. He had to leave them.

This wasn't about being a leader, helping the Rebellion survive or anything like that. Coleman had to do this for him. He had to save the Assassin or die trying.

The entire tunnel filled with the sounds of screaming, clashing swords and limbs being hacked off.

Coleman hugged Abbic and ran.

He had to find the Assassin.

He just hoped she was still alive.

CITY OF MARTYRS

CHAPTER 21
0.75 Days Left

I'm going to kill her so bad! I'm going to rip her stupid white faceless mask off!

I flew at her.

She whipped out her swords.

Our swords clashed.

Sparkes flew everywhere.

Lighting up the tunnel.

I kicked her.

She dodged.

The Maiden headbutted me.

Pain shot through me.

She jumped into the air.

Spinning and swirling.

Becoming a hurricane of death.

I couldn't block her attacks.

Her swords went wild.

Slicing through the air.

She sliced my black cloak and hood.

I rolled back.
She kept swirling.
I rolled back.
Again and again.
She landed.
Swinging her swords.
I raised mine.
Our swords clashed.
The impact jerked my hands.
My hands ached.
My bones cracked a little.
She didn't stop.
She kept swinging.
Swing after swing.
Unleashing rapid attack after attack.
I wasn't fast enough.
Her attacks were too quick.
Her swords whacked into mine.
My hands screamed in pain.
She kicked me.
I fell back.
She kicked again.
And again.
And again.
The Maiden leapt into the air.
Spinning around.
Kicking me in the head.

As I fell to the ground utter agony pulsed through my entire body. I had never fought someone as good as that before. I couldn't see any openings in her attacks.

She was masterful. She was a Goddess of fighting. She was unbeatable.

But I was an Assassin. I could and would find a way to kill her.

The Maiden of Light walked over to me pointing her swords at my chest. I raised my swords and weakly met hers.

My body ached with every breath, movement and thought. I needed help. I wished my Coleman was coming.

She smiled at me. "I did expect better from the great Assassin, First Daughter of the Overlord,"

The Maiden pressed her swords harder against mine. Making me hiss.

"Don't worry Assassin. You won't be alone with the Gods and Goddesses, a form of myself is killing Coleman as we speak. He will join you in the Afterlife,"

I surged forward.

Collapsing back down in agony. My body was never going to allow me to attack her like that again.

I forced my swords to press harder against hers as I stood up. My posture weak and pathetic but I was standing.

I could kill her still.

"Your Coleman will never win against me. Do you have a final message I could say to him?"

I swung her swords.

She dodged.

Disappearing.

She reappeared behind me. Slamming her fists into my back.

I fell to the ground as crippling pain filled me.

"Coleman won't die today," I said.

The Maiden of Light walked in front of me and grabbed me by the throat. Pulling me up to her level.

"I have sent my entire-"

The Maiden hissed, moaned and blood poured from her stomach.

I didn't care what did it.

I kicked her in the stomach.

She dropped me.

I jumped up.

Unleashing rapid of swings my swords.

She couldn't dodge them.

She was in too much pain.

My swords chomped onto her flesh.

Hacking lumps off.

Her blood painted the tunnel walls.

She moaned louder.

I jumped into the air.

Swirling.

Becoming my own hurricane of death.

My swirling swords sliced her throat.

I landed.

But as I landed I didn't see a dying body on the ground, the Maiden of Light was still like she had just completed some kind of glorious task. She seemed happy and her faceless mask just looked at me.

Her blood poured down her long white robes. Then it started to travel back into her wounds as they all healed themselves.

"That was a good try Jasper, The Masterful Assassin. But the only way to kill me is to break my mask. You can't do that,"

She punched me in the face.

Breaking my nose.

The bitch!

She swung her swords.

Slicing deep into my arms.

As I dropped my swords and placed my hands around myself to stop the bleeding, I could only stare up at the imposing white robed woman in front of me.

I was defeated. A living dead woman. A female assassin who was about to lose everything.

The Maiden placed both her swords on each side of my neck. Ready to slice it clear off.

You know my only regret is not telling Coleman I did love him. I actually did love that crazy strange man who seriously thought he could take on the Overlord with his friends.

I closed my eyes for the final blow.

Crippling pain faded into numbness as I had clearly lost too much blood and even my vision was starting to become black at the very edges.

The Maiden raised her swords. I prepared for the end.

Someone shouted something behind me.

I didn't know the words.
But the voice I knew that.
It was Coleman.
He had come for me!
My Coleman was alive!
I opened my eyes.
The Maiden raised her swords.
I wasn't going to die.
Coleman jumped over me.
Tackling the Maiden.
I grabbed my swords.
Screaming in pain.
I jumped up.
The Maiden whacked Coleman off her.
I thrusted my swords into her mask.
Shattering it.

As the Maiden of Light glowed bright for a final time, her white faceless mask shattered into millions of pieces and as they fell to the ground so did her long white robes.

But I wasn't shocked to see that there was not a body of flesh, blood or anything inside the robes. The robes fell just only air filled them because I knew that was what she was.

The Maiden of Light might have once been a person but that was a long time ago. Now she was ash, dust and air.

Purely magic for a soulless monster.

I felt more and more blood drip down my arms.

And as I collapsed into unconsciousness, there

was one thing that echoed in my mind from the Maiden.

The Hunters will come now.

CHAPTER 22
0 Days left

Commander Coleman stood on the cobblestone path in front of a long wooden jetty where in a few minutes his entire Rebellion would be stopping, unloading and joining him in their new home.

The air smelt amazing of sweet treats, caramels and cakes that the citizens of the City of Martyrs were baking as quickly as they could. Not because they needed to be made quickly but because the people here wanted to officially celebrate their new found freedom as soon as possible.

Even with the amazing warm air blowing past Coleman making a piece of his hair go crazy, he still loved every single little thing about the City now. This City was no longer a symbol of the Overlord's power, influence and corruption. For now it was a symbol of hope.

That is what Coleman had wanted.

As he watched the tens of massive wooden ships

that carried his Rebels towards the City come ever closer, wave after wave of excitement filled him. Because he could finally show them that he was their rightful leader.

He hadn't truly realised it before now but Coleman didn't feel like the Rebellion deserved him as leader, they deserved someone stronger, diplomatic and capable. And now Coleman could finally prove to himself and his Rebels that he was a mighty leader.

For whilst Coleman might have come here in doubt as a failed leader who wanted to show leadership and rebuild the Rebellion.

Now Coleman stood on the wonderful cobblestone path that would take his Rebels to their new home, base of operations and into the arms of their brothers and sisters in arms.

Coleman still didn't know how the Exiled Rebels had convinced Justin to aid Coleman in one of his darkest hours, but they had and to Coleman that was all that mattered. He had now had a real chance of fighting against the Overlord with new troopers and once again the Rebellion could and would grow into a force to be reckoned with.

Yet that was truly a problem for another day, Coleman had new things to do, explore and be happy about. He had to get to know the new Ruler of the City, Lord Castellan Richard. Coleman even offered to serve as an advisor as he tightened his kind grip on the City.

Then there were the matters of formulating a

plan against the Overlord now the Rebellion had a City under their control that they could use as a base to launch their attacks from.

In all honesty Coleman had no idea what message this would send to the Overlord, but he hoped, he really hoped that the fall of the City of Martyrs would send shockwaves through the Kingdom and inspire others to join Coleman and his Rebels.

It might have been a long chance but Coleman still had to have hope in these dark times. And it was they were, Coleman had no delusions that the Overlord wouldn't allow him to rule over one of his Cities for too long.

The Overlord would send an army to reclaim the City of Martyrs that was true, a certainty, an absolute. But that wouldn't be for days, weeks or months so Coleman just wanted to enjoy the next few days with his friends.

Coleman briefly looked towards the City with its thousands of burning candles, little white houses and now the amazing wreckage of the burnt out Cathedral for Coleman knew there was someone in the City he wanted to spend all his time with.

His beautiful Assassin with her amazing body, long black cloak and her deep eyes had almost died on this mission. She had been stolen from him and that had almost killed him inside.

Coleman never wanted to risk anything happening to her again without him telling the

Assassin how he felt.

Coleman took another amazing breath of the sweet scented air and promised himself that the moment that he could escape from his duties as a leader who had showed leadership to his people, freed a City and given his Rebels a home once more. Coleman was going to find the Assassin and confessed his love for her.

He just hoped that she felt the same way.

CHAPTER 23
0 Days Left

Sitting on a little window ledge belonging to a large brown office with its horrible little desk, chairs and some impressive art on the walls. I watched all the ships carrying the Rebels unload their passengers, cargo and even some animals into the City as the entire world seemed to become calm for a moment.

I might not have been entirely impressed by the sweet smells of treats, cakes and maybe even some liquorices (something I hated), I actually stood why everyone was baking so quickly.

After talking to some of the newly freed people as I made my way up here, I learnt that everyone had suffered for so long that they had actually given up hope believing that life could be different. And now their life was different, it seemed like some weird dream that they would wake up from soon.

I supposed I could understand that, I often get the feeling after a mission or a kill, those precious few seconds where the world seemed to slow down, focus and quieten down for a few moments so I can actually enjoy it all, before the next kill.

Of course I miss those moments which was I why I was sitting here, watching the peace flowing past me for as long as the world allowed.

The warm ocean breeze felt amazing against my long black cloak and hood and my swords were carefully placed behind me because I knew I wasn't in any danger, for now.

I'd be lying if I said the final words for the Maiden hadn't scared me. I didn't want the Hunters to come here, I had only come here to escape them because this was the only place in the Kingdom the Hunters did not dare come to.

Sliding my hand into my pocket my fingers tightened against a cold shard of the Maiden's mask, I supposed I was hoping that there was something in the mask that could help me against them when the time came.

I doubted it, but I needed anything.

At the end of the day, I was the Protectorate of the Rebellion and whilst I couldn't be happier I had helped to protect them by giving them a home and a new stream of recruits for their doomed mission. I was terrified of what was to come.

My father would never let me live inside a fallen City, you never know he might actually come for me himself. I wouldn't mind that. I had questions and I wanted, so badly, to ram my swords into him.

But that was definitely something to think about tomorrow.

My current theory why the Hunters couldn't come here is the Maiden of Light projected some kind of "holy" energy that was absorbed by the walls, roads and everything else in the City. So with her dead the energy would slowly start to disappear and only then would the Hunters come for me.

As the Overlord's puppets could say the Hunters, soldiers and other puppets were coming for the Rebellion all they wanted, but I knew the truth. My father was hunting me down for some reason I don't understand.

And that I feared was the key to stopping him.

The sound of gentle footsteps coming up behind me made me force those ideas away because they were problems for the future, right now I needed to just enjoy these few moments of precious silence before the world turned crazy again.

I hopped off the ledge into the office and saw a stunning man in front of me. I loved Coleman's dark emerald eyes, wonderful body and that killer smile that was far too seductive for its own good.

I grabbed my arms and pulled him closer. So close that I could feel his warm breath that smelt of sweets on my mouth. He wanted, longed to kiss me and I wanted him to, hard!

Coleman looked into my eyes. "When you were taken, it killed me. I couldn't handle it if anything happened to you. I don't know what I would do without you,"

He took a deep breath.

"I know you're an assassin, an amazing one, and you probably think it's a weakness and I'm pathetic but"-

I kissed him.

My lips softly pressed against his, I savoured the feeling of those soft sweet lips and now I knew what I had missed earlier. And I never ever wanted to miss him again.

I broke the kiss.

"I… I love you too,"

As Coleman pulled me closer and we continued kissing, letting our soft lips do the talking. I knew everything was complete and these precious moments of silence were going to last a lot longer than usual.

I had protected the Rebellion, freed an entire City and now I had the love of my life in my arms (and lips). That was the perfect ending to a great mission by my standards.

And now I was going to make these moments of silence count.

AUTHOR'S NOTE

Thanks for reading and I really hope you enjoyed the book. There will definitely be more books in the series so please check out City of Assassins Fantasy Stories at your favourite book retailer to find them.

For the people who like to know a bit about the creation of this novella, the entire idea for the book came from a history programme presented by Bettany Hughes, an amazing Historian. As well as on this programme they were exploring the history of Istanbul or better known as (at least in the history books) as Constantinople.

Therefore, I was watching the programme and Istanbul is a beautiful City with a massive golden dome in the centre which is a cathedral and inside it (I think) there was a special balcony for one of the Queens of Constantinople to pray away from the masses.

I'm not a 100% sure if that history stuff is correct but you get the general idea. The setting of this book was drawn from Istanbul and then I build the story on top of it.

Because the Rebellion was in tatters, Coleman felt useless and I wanted to explore the wider world of the City of Assassins Universe. So we explored some beliefs, power structures and even some magic within the world. As well as at least we got to explore the Assassin's past before and I'm really excited about exploring the world more.

So please check out the rest of the books at your favourite booksellers.

Thank you for reading and I'll see you in another book soon!

GET YOUR FREE AND EXCLUSIVE SHORT STORY NOW! LEARN ABOUT NEMESIO'S PAST!

https://www.subscribepage.com/fireheart

Keep up to date with exclusive deals on

CITY OF MARTYRS

Connor Whiteley's Books, as well as the latest news about new releases and so much more!

Sign up for the Grab a Book and Chill Monthly newsletter, and you'll get one **FREE** ebook just for signing up: Agents of The Emperor Collection.

Sign Up Now!

https://dl.bookfunnel.com/f4p5xkprbk

https://www.subscribepage.com/psychologyboxset

Thank you for reading.
I hoped you enjoyed it.
If you want a FREE book and keep up to date about new books and project. Then please sign up for my newsletter at
www.connorwhiteley.net/
Have a great day.

CHECK OUT THE PSYCHOLOGY WORLD PODCAST FOR MORE PSYCHOLOGY INFORMATION! AVAILABLE ON ALL MAJOR PODCAST APPS.

About the author:

Connor Whiteley is the author of over 60 books in the sci-fi fantasy, nonfiction psychology and books for writer's genre and he is a Human Branding Speaker and Consultant.

He is a passionate warhammer 40,000 reader, psychology student and author.

Who narrates his own audiobooks and he hosts The Psychology World Podcast.

All whilst studying Psychology at the University of Kent, England.

Also, he was a former Explorer Scout where he gave a speech to the Maltese President in August 2018 and he attended Prince Charles' 70th Birthday Party at Buckingham Palace in May 2018.

Plus, he is a self-confessed coffee lover!

OTHER SHORT STORIES BY CONNOR WHITELEY

Blade of The Emperor
Arbiter's Truth
The Bloodied Rose
Asmodia's Wrath
Heart of A Killer
Emissary of Blood
Computation of Battle
Old One's Wrath
Puppets and Masters
Ship of Plague
Interrogation
Edge of Failure
One Way Choice
Acceptable Losses
Balance of Power
Good Idea At The Time
Escape Plan
Escape In The Hesitation
Inspiration In Need
Singing Warriors
Dragon Coins
Dragon Tea
Dragon Rider
Knowledge is Power

CITY OF MARTYRS

Killer of Polluters
Climate of Death
Sacrifice of the Soul
Heart of The Flesheater
Heart of The Regent
Heart of The Standing
Feline of The Lost
Heart of The Story
The Family Mailing Affair
Defining Criminality
The Martian Affair
A Cheating Affair
The Little Café Affair
Mountain of Death
Prisoner's Fight
Claws of Death
Bitter Air
Honey Hunt
Blade On A Train
City of Fire
Awaiting Death
Poison In The Candy Cane
Christmas Innocence
You Better Watch Out
Christmas Theft
Trouble In Christmas
Smell of The Lake

Problem In A Car
Theft, Past and Team

Other books by Connor Whiteley:
The Fireheart Fantasy Series
Heart of Fire
Heart of Lies
Heart of Prophecy
Heart of Bones
Heart of Fate

City of Assassins (Urban Fantasy)
City of Death
City of Marytrs
City of Pleasure
City of Pleasure

Agents of The Emperor
Return of The Ancient Ones
Vigilance
Angels of Fire

The Garro Series- Fantasy/Sci-fi
GARRO: GALAXY'S END
GARRO: RISE OF THE ORDER
GARRO: END TIMES
GARRO: SHORT STORIES
GARRO: COLLECTION
GARRO: HERESY

GARRO: FAITHLESS
GARRO: DESTROYER OF WORLDS
GARRO: COLLECTIONS BOOK 4-6
GARRO: MISTRESS OF BLOOD
GARRO: BEACON OF HOPE
GARRO: END OF DAYS

Winter Series- Fantasy Trilogy Books
WINTER'S COMING
WINTER'S HUNT
WINTER'S REVENGE
WINTER'S DISSENSION

Miscellaneous:
RETURN
FREEDOM
SALVATION

All books in 'An Introductory Series':
BIOLOGICAL PSYCHOLOGY 3RD EDITION
COGNITIVE PSYCHOLOGY THIRD EDITION
SOCIAL PSYCHOLOGY- 3RD EDITION
ABNORMAL PSYCHOLOGY 3RD EDITION
PSYCHOLOGY OF RELATIONSHIPS- 3RD EDITION
DEVELOPMENTAL PSYCHOLOGY 3RD EDITION
HEALTH PSYCHOLOGY
RESEARCH IN PSYCHOLOGY
A GUIDE TO MENTAL HEALTH AND TREATMENT AROUND THE WORLD- A GLOBAL LOOK AT DEPRESSION
FORENSIC PSYCHOLOGY
THE FORENSIC PSYCHOLOGY OF THEFT, BURGLARY AND OTHER CRIMES AGAINST PROPERTY
CRIMINAL PROFILING: A FORENSIC PSYCHOLOGY GUIDE TO FBI PROFILING AND GEOGRAPHICAL AND STATISTICAL PROFILING.
CLINICAL PSYCHOLOGY

CONNOR WHITELEY

FORMULATION IN PSYCHOTHERAPY
PERSONALITY PSYCHOLOGY AND INDIVIDUAL DIFFERENCES
CLINICAL PSYCHOLOGY REFLECTIONS VOLUME 1
CLINICAL PSYCHOLOGY REFLECTIONS VOLUME 2
CULT PSYCHOLOGY
Police Psychology

www.ingramcontent.com/pod-product-compliance
Lightning Source LLC
LaVergne TN
LVHW011838060526
838200LV00054B/4087